Licket

CW00867150

and

Mixed-Up Fix

Written by
Maureen Haselhurst

Illustrated by
Claudia Venturini

"My Vroom Machine is really
MEAN!" boasted Lickety Kwick. "I'm
fast and funky."

It seemed a sure thing that boy racer,
Lickety Kwick, would be the new Junior
Racing Car Champion.

"Nobody can stop me!" said Lickety.

"Oh, yes I can!" said a voice. "I am Professor Kybosh, Master Meddler."

"And I can," echoed a second voice. "I'm Jinx, Assistant Meddler."

"And I can," repeated a third voice. "I'm Spike, Junior Assistant Meddler."

Better look out! There are Meddlers about.

3

4

Chapter One
Whopping Great Insects

It was race day and the Motorama
Race Track sizzled with excitement.
Engines screamed, crowds cheered and
flags flapped.

Camera crews were everywhere
and huge television screens showed
mega-sized pictures of the action.

Suddenly, someone in the crowd
shouted, "Hey, what are those? They
look like whopping great insects. I must
be seeing things!"

Everyone stared at the screen.

He wasn't the only one seeing
things. The cameras zoomed in
on a little creature that was
fooling around on the race
track. A second little creature
appeared. It sat down and
started to scratch.

"We've got aliens!"
shouted a joker, and
the crowd hooted
with laughter.

A third little creature darted onto the track, grabbed the other two and dragged them away.

"Boo! Spoilsport!" yelled the crowd, and they went back to watching the cars.

"That was very foolish, Spike!" snapped Professor Kybosh.

"If word gets out about us, they'll spoil all our fun," said Jinx, crossly.

"Sorry ... but it was great being on TV," grinned Spike.

"Come on," urged Jinx.

"We've got to find Lickety Kwick."

"There he is." Professor Kybosh pointed to a boy wearing racing overalls. He was standing near a super-duper car that gleamed in the sunshine.

"Wow!" shouted Spike. "That's the Vroom Machine!"

"Knockout!" gasped Jinx.

Professor Kybosh grinned. "I think I feel a meddle coming on," he said.

9

Chapter Two
The Big-Head

Lickety Kwick was talking to the press.

"How do you feel about the race, Lickety?" they asked.

"I'm cool with it. Forget the rest – I'm the **best**!"

"Well, good luck, Lickety."

"I don't need luck. I'm oozing with talent!" Lickety Kwick snapped, rudely.

"That boy is a big-head!" grunted Professor Kybosh. "He needs to be taught a lesson."

The Meddlers dodged across to the Vroom Machine.

"This will be a difficult meddle," said the Professor sternly, "so pay attention."

Spike pulled a face. "I'm not sure about this. We're being big-time spoilsports," he said.

"But, we're Meddlers, Spike," Jinx told him. "It's our job to make mischief and have fun doing it!"

"Okay, then," shrugged Spike. "Let's go for it!" He followed the others into the amazing engine of the Vroom Machine.

The Vroom Machine meddle was one of the best yet. They slid down pipes, they climbed up pulleys, they drilled holes and they filled holes. Jinx and Spike decided that meddling was the best job in the whole, wide world.

And, of course, the Professor sang.

The steering won't steer and
we've nobbled the gears.
There's gum in the brakes,
so he can't overtake.
We've squashed the wheels square,
he can't go anywhere.
When the engine goes
BOOM,
there'll be no more
VROOM!

Chapter Three
The Doggy Doo Animal Home

"Splendid! We've nobbled it," said Professor Kybosh and off he scuttled to watch the result of their mischief making.

As Spike crept out of the engine, he put his finger to his lips. "Listen," he whispered. "Lickety is giving another interview."

Lickety was standing in the middle of a crowd of reporters.

"Is it true that you give all your prize money to the Doggy Doo Animal Home, Lickety?" asked one reporter.

"Yep. I love animals even more than racing," said Lickety.

Botch put his paws over his head. Oh no! What had they done?

"What shall we do?" asked Spike.

"We'll have to undo the meddle," said Jinx.

"Professor Kybosh will go nuts!" Spike warned.

"Too bad," said Jinx. "I've got an idea, but we'll have to get inside Lickety's helmet to do it."

A few minutes later, Lickety Kwick
was sitting in the cockpit of the Vroom
Machine. He scratched his neck. It felt as
if spiders were crawling out of his helmet,
but it was too late to do anything about
it now. He had a race to win.

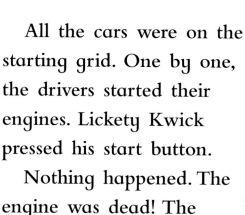

All the cars were on the starting grid. One by one, the drivers started their engines. Lickety Kwick pressed his start button.

Nothing happened. The engine was dead! The other cars revved and roared and spurted off.

"You'll have to pull out of the race!" shouted Lickety's mechanics.

Just then the radio in Lickety's helmet crackled and little voices started giving him instructions in his ear.

Chapter Four
Go For It!

"Great!" Lickety thought. Someone from his team was in radio contact, giving him instructions to give to the mechanics. "Tighten the poodle screw! Grease the foodle lever! Knock out the noodle nut!" he shouted to his mechanics.

They did all those things and then gave Lickety the thumbs up. He pressed the button again.

With an ear-splitting howl, the Vroom Machine started and took off. Around the track it charged, screaming through corners and skidding around bends. It tore along the straight, getting faster and faster. Lickety was catching up!

**zoom!
vroom!**

He began to pass the rest of the pack. The crowd went wild as he raced down the track, overtaking one car after another.

Lickety Kwick drove better and faster than he had ever driven before. He was driving like a real champion. And hearing weird songs over the radio in his helmet ...

"Faster, faster, faster!
Steady on the brake.
Come on, you can do it.
Okay — Overtake!"

The Vroom Machine stormed around the track like a tornado. There was only one car left to pass. Lickety was right behind it.

"Go for it!" yelled the voices in his helmet.

Lickety went for it. The Vroom Machine sprang forward and crossed the finish line first. He had done it! He had won. Lickety Kwick was the Junior Racing Car Champion.

"Go Lickety! Go Lickety!" chanted the crowd.

As Lickety took his helmet off, he noticed that the radio switch in the car was switched to **OFF.** So his team couldn't have given him the instructions or sung those weird songs. But if it wasn't them, then whose little voices had he heard inside his helmet?

Then he remembered the tiny creatures on the TV screen. "I wonder ..." thought Lickety Kwick.

Jinx and Spike scampered away, with Botch trotting at their heels.

"Psst!" whispered a voice in the shadows. It was Professor Kybosh and he looked crosser than cross.

"Oh dear," said Spike. "We're in for it."

"What happened?" asked the Professor.

"Er ... um ..." stammered Jinx.

"You unmeddled the meddle, didn't you?"

The Assistant Meddler and the Junior
Assistant Meddler nodded.

Professor Kybosh grinned his crafty grin. "I heard the interview and I know all about the Doggy Doo Animal Home. You two did the right thing. Well done!"

At that moment, Professor Kybosh spotted a cameraman crossing the track in their direction. "Now it's time *we* did some racing! Run for it!" he yelled. And off the Meddlers sped, in search of another amazing meddle.